A ZEAL OF ZEBRAS

Dedicated to Mauricio, Jackson, Luca, Freddie, Archie, Jack, and Toby.

Special thanks to honorary Woop, Lauren, and to Matthew.

A Zeal of Zebras

An Alphabet
of Collective Nouns

by WOOP STUDIOS

chronicle books·san francisco

An Aurora of Polar Bears

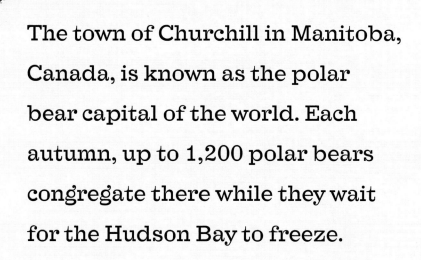

The town of Churchill in Manitoba, Canada, is known as the polar bear capital of the world. Each autumn, up to 1,200 polar bears congregate there while they wait for the Hudson Bay to freeze.

When the ice is solid, they travel across it to hunting grounds where they will fish for their favorite meal, ringed seals.

A Bale of Turtles

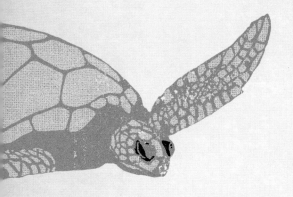

When the endangered Kemp's ridley sea turtles are ready to lay eggs, hundreds come ashore together and make nests with up to 200 eggs on one stretch of beach.

About two months later, tens of thousands of eggs hatch all at once, and the hatchlings immediately make their way to the sea.

A
BALE
OF TURTLES

B

A Caravan of Camels

Camels are known as the "ships of the desert," and for good reason. For centuries, desert people have used domesticated camels to transport heavy loads across difficult desert terrain.

A camel's strength, stamina, and big padded feet are all vital to keeping the caravan moving.

A Caravan of Camels

A Down of Rabbits

Wild rabbits live in underground holes called burrows. Eight to fifteen rabbits usually make their burrows close together, creating what is known as a warren. This helps to keep them safe, with more eyes and ears to look and listen for danger from predators.

An **Embarrassment** of Pandas

Seeing a group of pandas together would indeed be an embarrassment of riches, as giant pandas are solitary and rarely seen at all.

Less than 2,500 giant pandas are left in the wild. Because they are so rare and private, much of what we know about them comes from the study of zoo animals.

An *EMBARRASSMENT* of *PANDAS*

A Family
of Porcupines

While many porcupines are
solitary and spend most of
their time in trees, African
brush-tailed porcupines sleep
in caves or burrows, where
they gather in family groups
of about eight members.

These families even work
together as a group and share
their food.

A Family
of
PORCUPINES

F

A Galaxy of Starfish

Starfish, also known as sea stars, are usually seen in large numbers only when they are washed up on beaches after a storm.

However, some starfish may gather together when they are ready to reproduce, using environmental or chemical signals to coordinate with one another.

A GALAXY OF STARFISH

A Hum of Bees

All honeybees are social and cooperative insects. Each nest has a single queen, many workers, and, at certain stages in the colony cycle, drones.

Honeybee hives can contain as many as 40,000 bees—what a hum they would make together.

An
Implausibility
of Gnus

Every year, up to two million gnus
(or wildebeests) and other animals
journey in a massive migration from
Tanzania to Kenya and back again.

When the gnus must cross wide
rivers where predators await, they
gather into enormous herds and
rush across the waters all at once,
reducing their chances of being
caught by a hungry lion.

AN IMPLAUSIBILITY OF GNUS

A Journey of Giraffes

Giraffes are transient creatures, forming and dissolving groups regularly.

The size of a journey of giraffes is largely determined by food availability. When food is abundant, up to 40 giraffes may gather together. But when food is scarce, they break up into smaller family groups in order to spread out over a wider area.

A JOURNEY OF GIRAFFES

A Kaleidoscope of Butterflies

Up to 100 million monarch butterflies migrate across North America every year. At their winter destinations in California and Mexico, swarms of them can be seen completely covering trees.

The migration lasts so long that only monarchs born in late summer or early fall are likely to complete the entire round-trip.

K

A Kaleidoscope
OF
BUTTERFLIES

A Leap
of Leopards

Leopards spend most of their time
alone once they reach adulthood.

However, some species of leopards
are now so rare that it is almost
impossible to see even one of them,
let alone a group. For example, there
are only about 30 Amur leopards
now left in the wilds of Asia.

A Movement
of Moles

Don't be fooled into thinking you have a movement on your hands if you see a large number of mole hills in one area. Moles are very territorial and most likely all the holes are the work of one very busy mole.

a movement of moles

A Nest
of Crocodiles

Crocodiles rarely spend time together as a group and prefer a solitary life. Young crocodiles are vulnerable to larger crocodiles, so they are most likely to go it alone.

However, when food is abundant, crocodiles work together to hunt and share larger prey.

An Ostentation
of Peacocks

Peacocks are not just ornamental. They are quite useful, too. If you are looking for a beautiful alternative to a guard dog, look no further than an ostentation of peacocks—they make excellent "guards" and together will screech loudly when disturbed.

In the wild, their squawks warn other animals about approaching predators.

AN OSTENTATION OF *Peacocks*

A Pandemonium of Parrots

In the Amazon, groups of parrots can be found at "salt licks," naturally occurring deposits of salts and minerals that they eat to supplement their diets.

What a pandemonium it is with all their screeching!

A PANDEMONIUM OF **PARROTS**

A Quiver of Cobras

King cobras are the only snakes known to build nests. As many as 30 to 40 baby cobras are born in a nest made of vegetation gathered by their mother.

They are able to produce poisonous venom from the moment they hatch and are capable of killing right away.

A QUIVER of cobras

A Raft of Otters

Sea otters like to float on top of the water, and they will wrap themselves in kelp to keep from drifting out to sea. Although they usually forage alone, they often gather together in kelp beds to rest and sleep.

The largest raft ever seen numbered over 2,000 otters!

A RAFT of Otters

A Shiver
of Sharks

A lone shark is a frightening enough sight. Watching a large group of sharks demonstrate their intelligence by working together to herd a shoal of fish would certainly be enough to send a shiver down your spine.

A Troubling
of Goldfish

A solitary goldfish is likely to
be lonely because goldfish are
very social and prefer living
with other fish. Goldfish have
been known to interact with
any fish belonging to their
species—rubbing up against
one another and generally
having a lot of fun.

An Unkindness of Ravens

There are always six ravens living at the Tower of London, a tradition that started in the nineteenth century. Legend has it, if the ravens leave, the great White Tower will collapse and a terrible disaster shall befall England.

A Venom of Spiders

The majority of spiders in the world are solitary, but there are some species, aptly named social spiders, that live together in the thousands.

These spiders cooperate to hunt, build large webs, and raise their young.

A **Watch** of **Nightingales**

Though nightingales are most
often seen alone, scientists have
tracked their migration path
and discovered that they travel
each year from Northern Europe
to Senegal in West Africa.

A WATCH of NIGHTINGALES

W

An **Exaltation** of Larks

The skylark's song is one of nature's most complex and interesting. Males compete with each other for the attention of potential mates by showing off their singing and flying prowess.

The sound of this beautiful chorus is one of nature's magical noises.

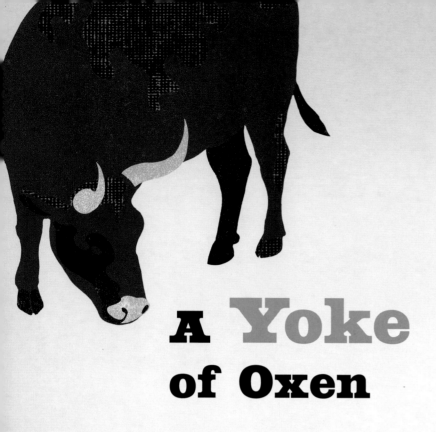

A Yoke
of Oxen

Oxen are used to this day in many countries to draw carts and to help farmers plow their fields. The strength and stamina of a yoke of oxen is impressive as is their ability to tackle difficult, uneven, and wet terrain.

One ox is strong—many oxen are formidably so.

A Zeal
of Zebras

A zebra's stripes are as unique
as human fingerprints.

When zebras gather together
on the African savanna, their
stripes help protect them
by confusing predators with
their dazzling patterns.

A ZEAL OF ZEBRAS

Woop Studios is a collective of four friends united by a love of graphic design, words, and images. They founded Woop Studios in 2010 to bring a unique and exciting angle to the fascinating world of collective nouns. Their first initiative was to launch an online gallery of limited edition prints. This book is the latest step in their journey.

To see the prints or find out more, please visit
www.woopstudios.com

Miraphora Mina and **Eduardo Lima** have spent the last decade working together as graphic designers on the Harry Potter film franchise. They recently formed their own graphic design studio, with aspirations to continue creating magic.

Harriet Logan is an award-winning photographer with extensive editorial and advertising experience. Mira and Harriet met at Bedales School when they were twelve years of age.

Mark Faulkner is the founder and head of innovation at Data Explorers, a company that couldn't have less in common with Woop Studios if it tried.

Library of Congress Cataloging-in-Publication Data available.

ISBN 978-1-4521-0492-8

Book design by Woop Studios.
Typeset in Farao.
The illustrations in this book were rendered in Adobe Photoshop.
Manufactured by C & C Offset, Longgang, Shenzhen, China,
in May 2011.

1 2 3 4 5 6 7 8 9 10

This product conforms to CPSIA 2008.

Chronicle Books LLC
680 Second Street, San Francisco, California 94107

www.chroniclekids.com

Chronicle Books publishes distinctive books and gifts. From award-winning children's titles, best-selling
cookbooks, and eclectic pop culture to acclaimed works of art and design, stationery, and journals, we craft
publishing that's instantly recognizable for its spirit and creativity. Enjoy our publishing and become part of
our community at www.chroniclebooks.com.